Foxwood Tales

presents the story of
Harvey
Rue and Willy in...

For William

By the same author

THE FOXWOOD TREASURE
ROBBERY AT FOXWOOD
THE FOXWOOD REGATTA

First published in 1986 by
André Deutsch Limited
105–106 Great Russell Street London WC1B 3LJ

British Library Cataloguing in Publication Data

Paterson, Cynthia
The Foxwood kidnap.
I. Title   II. Paterson, Brian
823'.914[J]   PZ7

ISBN 0–233–97920–4

Printed and bound by L.E.G.O., Vicenza, Italy

The Foxwood Kidnap

Written and Illustrated by

Cynthia & Brian Paterson

ANDRE DEUTSCH

'Look out,' shouted Rue Rabbit. His toboggan flew down the hill, just missing his two friends Harvey Mouse and Willy Hedgehog.

'That was the best yet,' he said, dusting off the snow.

'My turn,' said Willy, starting up the hill.

'It'll have to be the last,' said Harvey. 'It's getting late and it's a long walk home.'

It began snowing as they trudged past the old school house and came to the deserted railway station.

'I wish the Foxwood train still ran,' said Willy. 'What *did* happen to it?'

'I don't know,' said Rue. 'Vandals probably.'

'The rats are vandals,' said Willy quietly. Then he ran ahead. 'Come on, it's cold. Last one home's a vandal.'

'You're daft,' said Rue, chasing after him.

As Willy ran into the village, Badger postman barred his way.

'Steady there, young Willy,' he said. 'Where's your friend Rue? I've got a letter for him.'

'For me?' said Rue, catching them up. 'I don't get letters.'

'Who's it from?' asked Willy nosily.

Rue was already reading. 'It's from Uncle Henry, the inventor, he

wants me to visit him at once. He says he's made an amazing discovery which will help everyone in Foxwood.'

'What discovery?' asked Harvey.

'He doesn't say,' said Rue.

'You can't go alone,' said Willy, fishing for an invitation.

Rue laughed. 'All right,' he said, 'we'll all go.'

The next morning they loaded the toboggan for the journey.

'Steady on, Willy,' scolded Rue, 'we've got to haul this lot through the snow, you know.'

Willy waited till Rue turned away, then sneaked on a telescope he thought would be useful for spying.

The shortest way was through the great wood, so they made straight for it, crossing a deep ditch before entering its shadowy depths.

'I don't like this wood,' whispered Willy, 'it's spooky.'

A twig snapped in front of them. 'What's that?' muttered Rue.

As he spoke five of the biggest, meanest-looking rats they had ever seen emerged from the trees, blocking their way and poking their noses right into the friends' faces.

'What are you doing in our wood?' demanded their leader.

'Just taking a short cut to my Uncle Henry's windmill,' explained Rue. 'We can't stop now we're in a hurry.'

'He's important,' said Harvey, 'and brilliant.'

'Yes,' chimed in Willy, 'he's discovered something that will make us all rich.'

Too late, Harvey poked him in the back.

'Oh has he, indeed!' said the rat leader. 'How very interesting,' and, smiling nastily, he and his friends made off into the undergrowth.

Willy was almost crying. 'Sorry,' he said, 'I didn't mean to give our secret away. I told them the truth so they wouldn't hurt us.'

'You're forgiven,' said Rue cheerfully, 'but it's your turn to pull the toboggan.' And he and Harvey raced off up the hill.

When they arrived at the windmill they found the snow trampled with footprints.

Willy, by this time, had cheered up. 'Perhaps your uncle's giving a party to celebrate his discovery,' he said.

Rue pushed open the door. 'We're here, Uncle Henry,' he called.

But the mill was silent. There was no party and no Uncle Henry.

'What a welcome,' complained Willy. 'You'd think he'd be pleased to see us.'

The room they had entered was piled with all kinds of bits and pieces that looked as if they were waiting to be put together.

'What a lot of junk,' said Willy. Then he noticed some chairs and a table upturned in a corner, and broken cups and saucers. 'Looks as if they had a good party,' he added.

'More like a scuffle,' said Rue, 'I think I'll look around.'

As they crept upstairs they heard a faint sobbing coming from the room above. Cautiously, they went in and found a small rabbit cowering behind an old chest. Harvey pulled her out gently.

Rue was really worried by now. 'What's going on here?' he asked angrily. 'And where's Uncle Henry?'

'Wait a minute,' said Harvey, 'she can't talk until she's warmed up.'

They found a blanket, lit a fire and soon the little rabbit was comforted enough to tell her story.

'My name's Katie,' she began. 'I was lost in the snow when I came across this windmill. I was about to knock when I heard a dreadful commotion inside; shouting, and things being broken. I hid in the bushes and soon five rats came out, dragging an elderly hare by the heels. They disappeared into the woods. When they'd gone, I hid in here and waited for help. I'm so glad you've come,' she finished, wiping a tear.

'The rats!' exclaimed Rue. 'They were after Uncle Henry's discovery.'

Willy was shocked. 'It's all my fault,' he wailed. 'I told them.'

'Never mind about fault,' said Rue, 'our job is to rescue him.'

'It's too dark now.' Harvey was firm. 'We'd better wait till morning, and then we can follow them.'

Early next morning Willy hid the toboggan, but kept his telescope in case they needed it.

Rue led the way, with Katie behind him, Harvey next and Willy in the rear as they followed the rats' prints across fields, over walls and through bramble patches, until they came to a disused railway line where the going was easier.

It was Rue who spotted the towers, one on each side of an old tunnel. 'This could be their hiding place,' he said.

Proudly Willy produced his telescope. At last he could help.

'I spy with my little eye something beginning with R,' he said triumphantly.

'Rats,' cried Rue, Katie and Harvey together.

Willy pointed the telescope at a window near the top of one of the towers and gasped.

The face of a hare appeared for a moment.
'He's up there,' shouted Willy, 'Uncle
Henry. I saw him.'

'It's no good finding him if we
can't get him out,' said Rue.
'We could climb the tower,'
suggested Willy.

'And pigs might fly,'
said Harvey, but no
one laughed.

'*We* could fly,'
interrupted Katie.
'He was only
joking,' said Willy.
'But we *could* fly,'
insisted Katie.
'There's a balloon in
Uncle Henry's attic.
I found it when I was
trying to hide.'

'Katie, that's fantastic,'
began Willy. Then he
stopped. 'But we don't know
how to work it.'

'It's our only chance.' said Rue.
'I will if you will,' said Willy bravely.
'And me,' said Katie.

'We'd better hurry, it's getting late,' said Harvey.

As they raced back to the windmill the four friends worked out a rescue plan.
'I hope it works,' panted Harvey. 'We've never done anything like this before.'
'There's a first time for everything,' replied Rue, racing up the stairs to the attic.
'Here it is,' gasped Rue gazing in wonder at the huge balloon.
'How do we get it out?' asked Willy. 'It's a bit fat for those stairs!'
Harvey was looking puzzled. 'There must be a trap door somewhere.'
'What about this lever,' said Katie. She pulled it gently and a piece
of the roof creaked slowly open on a huge hinge.
'Brilliant, Katie,' said Rue. 'You and Uncle Henry.
Now everyone climb in and hold on tight
while I release the ropes.'

'I like this,' said Willy as they floated up into the grey sky. 'It's so easy.'

'Don't speak too soon,' answered Katie nervously.

By the time they had glided all the way back to the rats' hideout the sun had gone from the sky. Willy swept the ground with his telescope until he spotted the tower.

'Over there,' he pointed and guided Rue until they landed the balloon gently on the tower and tied it up.

Rue dashed down the stairs to find the room where the rats had locked up his uncle.

Harvey, Katie and Willy waited impatiently.

'I wish they'd hurry up,' sighed Katie. 'The rats must see the balloon soon, and they are too strong for us.'

'We'll give them another few minutes,' said Harvey. 'But if the rats come we'll have to leave Rue to find his own way back.'

Meanwhile Rue had found the room where his uncle was imprisoned. Taking a key hanging nearby, he unlocked the door and went in.

'Rue, my boy!' cried Uncle Henry delightedly when he saw him.

'Sssh,' said Rue. 'Come on, we haven't much time.'

As Uncle Henry turned towards the door he stopped to pick up several bits and pieces. 'Mustn't forget these,' he said.

On the roof of the tower Harvey turned to Willy. 'We can't wait any longer,' he said. 'I'm sure I can hear the rats coming.'

As Willy turned to untie the rope Rue arrived panting. 'I've got him,' he gasped, and they all scrambled into the basket.

'Well done, everyone,' said Uncle Henry as the balloon rose slowly into the air. 'I couldn't have done better myself.'

'Look out,' shouted Willy suddenly. 'They're here.'

The rats ran onto the roof and grabbed at the balloon's swinging rope. Willy released a sandbag which burst over their heads.

'We'll get you for this,' shouted a rat, shaking his fist.

'No chance,' jeered Willy, 'we've beaten you this time.' And they sailed safely away into the winter sky, leaving their enemies behind.

They settled down to enjoy their flight, gliding peacefully through the crisp air, until Uncle Henry pointed to an old shed on the ground beneath them and said, 'Land beside that if you can.'

But the trees made things difficult and instead they landed with a crash and a bump on the old shed roof.

'Is this your secret hideout?' asked Willy climbing down.

'Not exactly,' replied Uncle Henry, 'but it's where I keep my secret discovery.'

'Oh,' said Willy disappointed. 'I thought the balloon was your discovery.' He was dreaming of how much money he could make from giving balloon rides.

'Oh no,' said Uncle Henry, 'that's just a toy. Now wait while I get these doors open and you'll see something really spectacular.'

As they entered the shed, they could hardly believe their eyes. They were looking at the most beautiful train they had ever seen.

'Do you like her?' asked Uncle Henry proudly. 'She's the Red Fox, my real discovery. She was Foxwood's train years ago, then she was stolen by vandals and left to rot until I found her and rebuilt her. She's not quite in working order yet because I'm short of a few bits, but I hope the things I brought from the rats' tower will do the trick.'

'I'll get them for you, uncle,' said Rue eagerly. 'She's fantastic, isn't she?'

They worked hard through the night, taking turns to have a little sleep. Finally, as the sun rose, everything was ready.

'Stoke up,' called Harvey, 'all we need now is full steam.'

Uncle Henry pulled a lever, there was a long hiss of steam, the wheels turned slowly and the Red Fox came to life.

'We're off,' cheered Willy. 'This is even better than flying.'

'Wait a minute,' called Uncle Henry, 'I've one last job to do.'

'You think of everything,' said Rue as he helped Uncle Henry to fix a snow plough to the front of the Red Fox.

With a puff and a toot the Red Fox moved forward through the snow.

Katie was enjoying herself. 'This is fun,' she said happily, polishing the brasswork until it glistened.

'Look out ahead,' warned Rue suddenly.

Willy whipped out his telescope. 'Rats!' he said. 'Four of them, charging towards us up the track.'

'Now they've found us they'll want to fight,' said Rue.

'They'll have to catch us first,' laughed Uncle Henry. 'Come on, everyone, more coal on the fire.'

With that he pulled out the throttle, the Red Fox hurtled forwards and the rats jumped for their lives.

Buried in a flurry of snow, the rats could only stare in disbelief.

'We're through,' said Katie. 'They'll never catch us now. We're safe.'

'There's a long way to go yet,' said Harvey. 'Look at all the snow on the track in front of us.'

'Leave that to my snow plough,' said Uncle Henry, 'and just enjoy the ride. In the meantime there's a kettle and things in there. Melt some snow and we'll have a pot of tea. It's a long way home.'

After many miles, Willy called out, 'Foxwood ahead.'

The sound of the Red Fox had already reached the village, and when they pulled into the old station there was quite a crowd gathered on the platform to greet them. The villagers, especially the older ones who remembered the Red Fox, waved happily, although they could hardly believe they were seeing the old train again.

'The old Red Fox,' shouted Grandpa Hedgehog. 'I don't believe it.'

After the excitement had died down and everyone had been told all about Uncle Henry's great discovery, he announced that he would guard the Red Fox himself that night just in case the rats came back.

'Life will be boring again now,' moaned Willy.

'Rubbish,' said Rue. 'We've got a job for life. There's the track to repair, the station to paint . . .' he yawned. 'I'm off to bed. See you in the morning, Willy.'

Willy's mother invited Katie to stay for the night as it was too late to go home. Willy kindly said she could have his bed while he slept in the spare bunk.

Willy had a wonderful dream about finding an old train and riding on it. But the best part was in the morning, when he woke up to find it had all been true.